D0819594

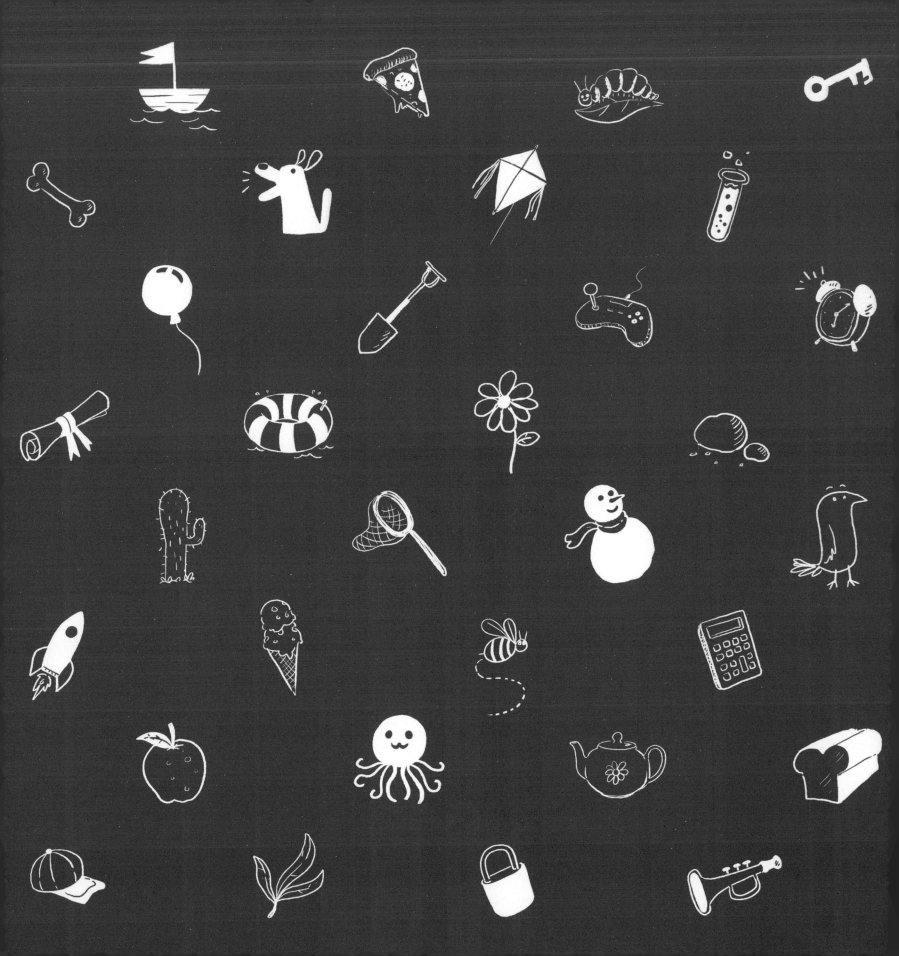

The Whole HOLE Story

Vivian McInerny

Illustrated by Ken Lamug

VERSIFY · HOUGHTON MIFFLIN HARCOURT · Boston New York

To tellers of stories, which is not the
same as fibbers. But close. —V. M.

To Keichi, Nikko, and Ian. Dream big, imagine
endlessly, and create with conviction. —K. L.

Versify is an imprint of Houghton Mifflin Harcourt Publishing Company.

hmhbooks.com

The art for this book was created with imagination, pencil, paper, and some computer magic.
The text was set in Brandon Grotesque.

Designed by Whitney Leader-Picone

Library of Congress Cataloging-in-Publication Data
Names: McInerny, Vivian, author. | Lamug, Kenneth Kit, 1978– illustrator.
Title: The whole hole story / Vivian McInerny ; illustrated by Ken Lamug.
Description: Boston : Versify, Houghton Mifflin Harcourt, 2021. | Audience:
Ages 4 to 7. | Audience: Grades K–1. | Summary: "Zia imagines what might happen if
the hole in her pocket became big enough to fall right through." —Provided by publisher
Identifiers: LCCN 2019042923 (print) | LCCN 2019042924 (ebook) |
ISBN 9780358128816 (hardcover) | ISBN 9780358129486 (ebook)
Subjects: CYAC: Holes—Fiction. | Imagination—Fiction.
Classification: LCC PZ7.1.M43528 Who 2021 (print) |
LCC PZ7.1.M43528 (ebook) | DDC [E]—dc23
LC record available at https://lccn.loc.gov/2019042923
LC ebook record available at https://lccn.loc.gov/2019042924

Manufactured in China
SCP 10 9 8 7 6 5 4 3 2 1
4500805632

Zia had a hole in her pocket.

That didn't stop her from stuffing small things in it, such as gumballs, sparkly rocks, and jumpy frogs. Sometimes they stayed. Sometimes they fell through and got lost. Zia paid no attention.

The hole in her pocket grew bigger . . .

and bigger . . .

until one day Zia herself fell right through.

This, of course, was rather peculiar.

Zia might have been afraid except that this was

an imaginary hole, so it could only be as scary as she

allowed, which was, in this case, not scary at all.

"I hate scary stories," said Zia.

She sat quietly at the bottom, where holes and thoughts run deep, and considered what to do with such an obviously wonderful hole. The best ideas usually came to her when she went fishing.

"A fishing hole is just what I need," Zia decided.

She filled the hole with water from the garden hose. She found her fishing pole, convinced a wiggly worm to sit on the hook as bait, and waited.

After some time, she felt a nibble. Zia reeled in a fat fish
with bulgy eyes and fancy fins. The fish smiled a fish-lip smile.

The only thing better than catching a fish, as far as Zia was concerned, was letting a fish go.

The fish flipped a fin in thanks, which was polite but rather drippy.

Fortunately, Zia wore her swimsuit beneath her clothes, so she knew just what to do next.

"I officially declare this a swimming hole," she said.

Zia did a cannonball because she liked to make a splash. She did the dog paddle and the butterfly because she liked animals. She floated on her back just because.

Looking up, Zia spotted one fluffy cloud shaped like a thirsty lion.

"He needs a watering hole," Zia said.

The lion came down from the blue sky and lickety-lapped up the water. An anteater, two giraffes, and a slithery snake soon followed.

The greedy lion, hoping to scare away the other animals, told them that a green crocodile with sharp teeth lived deep down in the watering hole.

ZIA's WATERING HOLE

The giraffes found the lion's
story difficult to swallow.

"Do you know what bugs
me?" asked the anteater
between snacks. "I believe
the lion's lying."

"Sounds like nothing but a tale to me," hissed the snake,
who was really not much more than a tail himself.

Tired of their bickering, Zia held her nose, dove down to the bottom of the hole, and pulled the plug. The water swirled around like a wet tornado. Zia swirled around with it. Fortunately, she was too big to go down the drain herself.

Unfortunately, Zia found herself sitting at the bottom of an empty hole. An empty, muddy hole.

So, she made one hundred and twenty-seven mud stairs and more pies than she could count and climbed right out.

Then she sat on the edge, feet dangling, certain that such a big hole must be useful in a big way.

"Think big," Zia told herself.

And as is often the case when thoughts turn big, they turn to elephants. Zia decided to catch one. She covered the hole with her favorite blanket and put six peanuts in the middle.

FREE PEANUTS
ELEPHANTS ONLY

After some time, an elephant came lumbering along, spotted the peanuts, stepped onto the blanket, and—*crash*—he was caught.

Zia was delighted.

The elephant was not.

Only the cruelest person can ignore the tears of an elephant and Zia was not the least bit cruel. She tried to help the elephant out of the hole, but he was too heavy.

Instead, she decided to help the elephant dig the hole

deeper and deeper, all the way to other side of the world.

They said goodbye in India, which is really where the elephant belonged anyway.

"Send me a postcard," Zia said.

Zia did so like to get mail.

"I won't forget," the elephant promised.

In a hurry to get home, Zia jumped back down the hole. She fell fast. She fell faster. She fell so fast, her hair fell up.

She arrived back home just as the first snowflakes began to fall. And this was rather peculiar as it was July. But Zia was not one to complain about snow at any time of year.

Zia filled the hole with water for a second time. Then she laced up her ice skates and made perfect figure eights on the frozen surface.

Unfortunately, the blades were too sharp and they cut a hole in the ice. But Zia understood that a hole with a hole could be doubly good fun.

She lifted the hole, tipped it onto its side,

and rolled it down the street,

whacking it along with a stick.

It rolled along quickly until she came to the bottom of a steep hill. Then the hole rolled backwards . . .

and fell right on top of her.

And there it stayed . . .

for two whole pages.

After a while, Zia crawled out and, once again, considered what to do with the hole. A sensible girl who knew to avoid danger whenever possible, Zia circumvented the hole, which is a fancy way to say she walked around it. Because the hole was round, Zia found herself walking in circles. And because Zia liked to run in circles, she soon caught up with herself.

"This is making me dizzy," she said to herself.

Her self agreed.

Zia climbed up a nearby
tree for a rest.

From high up in the branches,

the hole looked rather small.

So small, in fact . . .

Zia thought she could fit the
whole thing in her pocket.

And so she did.